THE RIGHT PLACE FOR ALBERT

by **Daphne Skinner** • Illustrated by **Deborah Melmon**

THE KANE PRESS / NEW YORK

Library of Congress Cataloging-in-Publication Data

Skinner, Daphne.
The right place for Albert / by Daphne Skinner ; illustrated by Deborah Melmon.
p. cm. — (Mouse math)
"With fun activities!"—Cover.
Summary: On Albert's first crumb-hunting trip to the People Kitchen, his big sister Wanda helps him
look for a hiding place to avoid Groucho the cat. Introduces the mathematical concept of one-to-
one correspondence.
ISBN 978-1-57565-438-6 (pbk. : alk. paper) — ISBN 978-1-57565-439-3 (e-book) —
ISBN 978-1-57565-446-1 (library reinforced binding : alk. paper)
[1. Mice—Fiction. 2. Mathematics—Fiction.] I. Melmon, Deborah, ill. II. Title.
PZ7.S6277Ri 2012
[E]—dc23
2011048822

1 3 5 7 9 10 8 6 4 2

First published in the United States of America in 2012 by Kane Press, Inc.
Printed in the United States of America
WOZ0712

Book Design: Edward Miller

Mouse Math is a trademark of Kane Press, Inc.

Visit us online at **www.kanepress.com**

 Like us on Facebook
facebook.com/kanepress

 Follow us on Twitter
@KanePress

Dear Parent/Educator,

"I can't do math." Every child (or grownup!) who says these words has at some point along the way felt intimidated by math. For young children who are just being introduced to the subject, we wanted to create a world in which math was not simply numbers on a page, but a part of life—an adventure!

Enter Albert and Wanda, two little mice who live in the walls of a People House. Children will be swept along with this irrepressible duo and their merry band of friends as they tackle mouse-sized problems and dilemmas. (And sometimes *cat-sized* problems and dilemmas!)

Each book in the **MOUSE MATH**™ series provides a fresh take on a basic math concept. The mice discover solutions as they, for instance, use position words while teaching a pet snail to do tricks or count the alarmingly large number of friends they've invited over on a rainy day—and, lo and behold, they are doing math!

Math educators who specialize in early childhood learning used their expertise to make sure each title would be as helpful as possible to young kids—and to their parents and teachers. Fun activities at the end of the books and on our website encourage children to think and talk about math in ways that will make each concept clear and memorable.

Check out these titles in
MOUSE MATH:

The Right Place for Albert
One-to-One Correspondence

The Mousier the Merrier!
Counting

Albert's Amazing Snail
Position Words

Albert Keeps Score
Comparing Numbers

And visit
www.kanepress.com/
mousemath.html
for more!

As with our award-winning Math Matters® series, our aim is to captivate children's imaginations by drawing them into the story, and so into the math at the heart of each adventure. It is our hope that kids will want to hear and read the **MOUSE MATH** stories again and again and that, as they grow up, they will approach math with enthusiasm and see it as an invaluable tool for navigating the world they live in.

Sincerely,

Joanne Kane

Joanne E. Kane
Publisher

It was a big day for Albert. He was going to the People Kitchen for the very first time.

His big sister, Wanda, was taking him there.

The kitchen was full of wonderful treats.

But it was dangerous, too.

The people didn't like mice.

Neither did the cat.

Each mouse had his own hiding place in the kitchen. Albert had to find one for himself.

"You know the rule," said Wanda.

"One mouse, one hiding place," said Albert.

"Right," said Wanda. "Before the rule we
had problems. . . .

"But now if there's trouble, every mouse knows
just where to hide."

That made sense to Albert.

"Ready?" asked Wanda.

"Ready!" said Albert, and out they went.

The kitchen was very, very big.

"There must be a million hiding places in here!" said Albert.

"Let's find one for you!" said Wanda.

Albert pointed to the cookie jar.
"How about behind there?"

"Maybe," said Wanda. "Let's see."

But the cookie jar
was taken.

Cookies

Hi, guys!

"There?" said Albert.
But the oven mitt was
taken, too.

NIBBLES

NOSHES

Tiny Little Treats

"Under there?"
asked Albert.

"Sorry," said Wanda. "The bookshelf is mine."

"Can't we share it?" he asked.

"Repeat after me, Albert," said Wanda.
"One mouse, one hiding place."

"Okay, okay," he said. "I get it."

NIBBLES

NOSHES

Tiny Little Treats

Albert and Wanda
looked high . . .

. . . and low.

Inside the cuckoo clock . . .

Hi, Albert!

. . . and behind the spice jars.

ACHOO!

But every spot was taken.

"One mouse, one hiding place is harder than I thought," said Albert.

Just then he heard a loud *thump thump thump*. Footsteps!

"Uh-oh!" said Wanda. "People are coming! We have to hide!"

The footsteps came closer.

"Try that thing on the counter!" called Wanda as she ran to the bookshelf.

"WHAT thing?" Albert cried.

Then he saw it—the roll
of paper towels.

Albert hurried over,
hoping it wasn't taken.

It wasn't!

Even better, the sound of footsteps faded away.

"I'm safe!" thought Albert.

But he was wrong.

CAT!

A paw tried to reach him. It missed.

This is NOT a good hiding place!

Albert was bumped and thumped.

The cat hit the roll,
and it went flying.

The roll bounced—
and stopped.

Then Albert
had an idea.

He pushed and kicked inside the roll until it
tumbled to the floor.

Just as he hoped, it landed right in front of the refrigerator—

and Albert squeezed underneath.

The place *wasn't* taken. It was his!

A minute later he heard footsteps.
Then somebody was scolding the cat.

You naughty, naughty boy!

When the kitchen was quiet again,
everybody came out of hiding.

The rule rules!

One mouse, one hiding place. YAY!

NIBBLES

NOSHES

Tiny Little Treats

Wanda ran to Albert. "You were so brave!" she said. "Are you okay?"

"I'm great!" squeaked Albert. "And—

"I finally found what I was looking for!"

The Right Place for Albert supports children's understanding of **one-to-one correspondence**, an important topic in early math learning. Use the activities below to extend the math topic and to reinforce children's early reading skills.

🐭 ENGAGE

Remind children that the cover of a book can tell them a lot about the story inside.

▶ Invite children to look at the cover as you read the title. Ask: *Where are Wanda and Albert? Do you see any other mice on the cover? Where are they? What do you think this story is about?* (You may wish to record their predictions and refer back to them at the end of the story.)

🐭 LOOK BACK

▶ Before re-reading the story aloud, ask children if they've ever been to a strange new place. Invite them to tell about their experiences. How did they feel about going there?

▶ As you read, draw children's attention to the text and the illustrations. Refer children to pages 4 and 5. Talk about how Albert feels at the beginning of the story. (For example: *Albert is frightened. He feels excited.* And so on.)

▶ Turn to pages 6 and 7. Ask: *What are Albert and Wanda thinking about? What does Wanda want Albert to remember?* Invite children to say the rule aloud. Look at page 8. Have children tell why they think the rule is important.

▶ Direct children to page 13. Ask: *What does Wanda tell Albert when he asks if he can share the bookshelf with her? Why do you think Wanda wants Albert to repeat the rule?* (Possible response: So he won't forget it.)

🐭 TRY THIS!

You will need half an egg carton and eight plastic eggs. (Or download and print pictures of a carton and eggs: www.kanepress.com/mousemath-onetoone.html.)

▷ Begin by asking children if they have ever tried to fit too many of something into a container. Invite them to describe what happened.

▷ Display the egg carton and eggs. Ask: *Can we put all these eggs in the carton? How many of you think we can?* Record the number of yeas and nays. (You may wish to remind children of the rule: one mouse, one hiding place.)

▷ Invite children to take turns placing one object into each slot in the carton. When they have finished, ask: *How many eggs did we put into the carton? Did we follow the rule? How do you know?*

🐭 THINK!

You will need a sheet of paper with drawings of four snails and four hiding places (see the sentences below). Prepare an illustration and give a copy to each child, or download and print readymade activity sheets from www.kanepress.com/mousemath-onetoone.html. Have each child cut out the snail pictures.

▷ Explain to children that they are going to put the snails in their hiding places! Remind them of Wanda's rule. Then ask: *What do you think our rule should be?*

▷ Read each sentence below aloud. Tell children to glue each paper snail in its hiding place. **Bonus:** You may want to have children number the snails.

1. The hiding place for this snail is **under** the leaf.
2. The hiding place for this snail is **behind** the pinecones.
3. The hiding place for this snail is **inside** the log.
4. The hiding place for this snail is **on top of** the cuckoo clock.

▷ Ask: *Are all four of your snails hiding? How many snails do you have in each hiding place?* Encourage children to tell stories about their snails.

◆ FOR MORE ACTIVITIES ◆
visit www.kanepress.com/mousemath-activities.html